The
Gift of the
King's
Jeweler

THE GIFT OF THE KING'S JEWELER

Steven L. Peck

Covenant Communications, Inc.

Covenant

Cover illustration *The Liahona* © Ken Corbett

Cover design copyrighted 2003 by Covenant Communications, Inc.

Published by Covenant Communications, Inc.
American Fork, Utah

Printed in Canada
First Printing: November 2003

10 09 08 07 06 05 04 03   10 9 8 7 6 5 4 3 2 1

ISBN 1-59156-277-5

For Lori

Forward

The origin of the Liahona is given nowhere in scripture. All we know is that it was "prepared by the hand of the Lord" (Mosiah 1:16). Whether that preparation meant that it was made by God, angels, or man is unknown. We know only how it was used once it mysteriously appeared in front of Lehi's tent about 2,600 years ago. Since that time we have come to cherish it as a remarkable symbol of the spirit in our lives and as a metaphor for finding our way through our own wildernesses. I hope that I offend no one by using the origin of this sacred device as a backdrop for my story. This is *not* a treatise meant to hypothesize on those origins, and I do not mean to offer speculation on how the Liahona works or where it came from. It is instead a story about faith and trusting the Lord in finding our own missions here on earth, and how, while following our own liahonas, things often do not turn out the way we planned.

Chapter One

Az could hear his wife Iltani in the next room trying to coax the embers of last night's cooking fire to life. His youngest son was trying courageously to help, and his short puffs sounded full of pluck but ineffectual next to his wife's slow, steady, whistlelike blow. Az fell back on his mat, not yet ready to begin the day. His eyes stared at the rough log-pole beams that supported the ceiling, and he tried to reconstruct the baffling dream that had come once again to harass his sleep.

In it, a wheel was spinning, round and round—turning brilliantly in his mind. It was made of beautiful brass, bathed in light, with words and pieces of words flying off the wheel at an indescribable speed. Then a piercing voice cried, "You are called to an odyssey of wonder and light! Forge!" Suddenly, the dream shifted softly, running forward as if Az had been brought over a great journey, across vast distances and over many lifetimes. He had the impression that he had been thrown far into the future in a single breath, which left him only lingering shards of forgotten memories. Suddenly, in the dream, he found himself outside. The night air seemed cool but not cold. It was early springtime; the sky was alight with stars so bright that he realized it must be a dream. But one star—there were no words to describe it—one star shone with such brilliance it was like none he had ever seen, or even imagined. Next to him stood men of stunning wealth and power; perhaps wise counselors of some great king, perhaps great prophets or seekers of wisdom. One turned to him, smiled and asked, "What gift will you bring?"

He always woke up after the voice, with his heart beating and his breast filled with a peace and a lightness that almost left him laughing. These feelings were replaced, however, with a shallow melancholy as he realized that he could not understand what God was trying to tell him; for surely it was God. Who else could have sent a dream so beautiful? What did it mean?

Az smelled the modest cooking fire almost at the same time he heard its welcoming crackle. That was the signal for the rest of the household to arise. His son-in-law would soon be at the bellows heating the kiln to the tem-

perature Az would need to melt the lumps of
metal he would turn into art—gold and silver
that would adorn the neck, arms, and legs of
the king and his consorts, and others in his
favor. His mother would soon be grinding
wheat, which his wife would turn into bread.
His oldest daughter would help polish the
gold amulet he had made yesterday for the
king's concubine, while her son—his grand-
son—played outside in the fields. His
youngest daughter would spend the day
watching her father, standing a respectable
distance away, but never taking her eyes off
him as he molded, hammered, and shaped the
metals into adornments for royalty. It was
clear she loved the forge. She loved the smells.
She loved watching the glowing metals pulled
fiery-hot from the kiln and transformed, as if
by magic (by her father's steady, patient
hands), into works of staggering beauty and
delight. She would watch him as he slowly,
and without a wasted move, made chains of
gold or silver link by link, sometimes taking
weeks. Though her attention was flattering,
Az worried about her. She took no interest in
the labor which women were supposed to do.
Nonetheless, he enjoyed his little "Melon-
Flower," as he called her, who seldom left his
forge.

The day was beginning. One of the king's guards poked his shaggy head in and asked for a drink of water from Az's mother. She let out a long sigh and slowly meandered to the water urn balancing snugly in the corner.

"Why can't the king send water to quench the thirst of these rabble? I have to carry load after load of water from the well just so these refugees from the army can sit outside my door gambling!"

"Give him the water, Mother! They've worked hard all night keeping you safe from murderers and thieves," Az called out cheerfully from his bed. He was never quite comfortable with guards stationed around his home—a necessary evil for the king's jeweler.

"Safe!" His mother humphed. "I've no doubt of that. Their snoring would have kept out Enki himself. Ishtar be praised that we get any sleep in our *safety.*"

The soldier laughed and went outside with the water.

Az stepped from the room where he slept, then looked at his mother unhappily.

"Mother. Please don't say that name in my house."

His mother looked at him and spat into the fire. "Ishtar," she said, staring at him. "Ishtar! Ishtar! Ishtar!"

Az shook his head. "Mother, please."

"You come back from your travels with a new god—fine. But don't expect me to fall on my knees before your Hebrew idol. Ishtar has watched over me since I was a little girl. And no god, especially one whose name you don't know, will take her place!"

Az looked at her coldly, then softened. "Mother, you are lucky that the God I worship teaches love and patience. You don't understand. This is not just a new god. It is *the* God. The only one. The one true God who made the heavens and the earth."

"Pshaw!" His mother snorted. "Anu made all that."

"No mother. It was the One God. I know that because His Spirit has changed me. I am a new person . . ."

"I've no doubt of that. Since your trip south you have become impossible to live with!" She gave an ironic laugh. "And you've taken our enemy's god no less! What would the king do if he knew that, eh?"

"I don't care what the king knows." With that Az threw his hands into the air and walked back into his room. A soft red light came through a hole in the ceiling as the morning sun stretched above the rooftops of Babylon. The sound of a rooster cut through the cool morning air and, almost as punctually, the voice of his neighbor arguing with his two wives rose above the sound of ass hooves clipping their way to market. The tinkling of bells rushing hurriedly past his door confessed that the temple harlots were on their way to Ishtar's shrine. Az thought about his "new" God. The Creator of the earth, the stars, the Euphrates, birds, and even the pig—whose hocks he could no longer enjoy as a worshiper of this Lord of Lords. What a wondrous God this was! Az fell on his knees. He faced Jerusalem to remember the Temple and the place of his conversion and prayed. He prayed for strength to endure his mother's complaints. He prayed for his family. He prayed that there would be no war between Babylon and the southern Kingdoms, whose God he had embraced. But mostly he prayed for help in understanding the dream. The dream of the spinning rings, the changing words, and the brightest of stars.

⇢ Chapter Two ⇠

The guard loudly invaded the foundry and stood rigidly in an obvious place until Az looked up from the bracelet he was gently tapping into shape.

"The king's agent is here and wishes to speak to you at once," the guard said officially.

Az sighed in acceptance and said, in a rote voice that belied his words, "Tell him I am glad he honors my humble abode. I will attend him presently."

He picked up the gold bracelet he was fashioning and placed it in a tray that he slid into a cooler part of the kiln to keep it from melting, but still malleable, until he returned. He came into the main room of his house wiping his hands on his leather apron. Everyone had gathered in the room to stare silently at the powerful man who had come under their roof. Even after a year of being the king's jeweler, Az still found the presence of such a man intimidating.

"Good day to you. I am the agent of Nebuchadnezzar, Glorious King of Babylon, Worshiper of Marduk, and Builder of the sacred gardens of Nabu. I've come to obtain the amulet for the king's favorite concubine." He then added ominously, "And to be sure the king, our God, is not being cheated."

The king's agent trusted no one, and he treated everyone with intense suspicion. He was powerful, knew it, and acted accordingly, polite conversation abandoned.

Az's oldest daughter brought the gold amulet and handed it quickly to one of the agent's aides. With flair, the eunuch theatrically wrapped it in an elegant purple cloth, then with a deep bow, delivered it to the king's agent. He in turn held it up to the light and inspected it closely. Az's wife held her breath as he turned it over repeatedly, inspecting it closely with his narrow, penetrating eyes. Az did not worry. He knew the quality of his work. He had spent five years in Egypt learning from the greatest metalsmiths in the world. He did not fear this odious man or the king he worshiped as a god.

"The quality will be acceptable to his highness, our God. You are lucky he is patient with weakness."

Az bowed, but said nothing.

"The scales and the touchstone!" One of the agent's aides, another large eunuch, stepped forward, then, drawing items from a series of small leather bags, constructed a balance. He placed it on a table that another attendant had carried into the house. The king's agent placed the amulet on one side and gold weights on the other. The amulet ascended, then stopped exactly opposite the gold weights. The two sides were perfectly balanced. The eunuch then made a small streak with the touchstone on the inside of the amulet, and another on a small piece of gold he had taken from his pouch. He showed the agent the two streaks held side by side for comparison.

The agent scowled. "We have not yet detected your cheating. Remember, when we have, you will be killed."

Az bowed but, unobserved, rolled his eyes in disgust.

"The king has another task. He saw a circlet on one of the princes of Israel, the son of the captive Jehoiakim. You saw it no doubt when they were paraded through the streets at the festival of Shamash?"

"I saw it, Lord."

"The king desires one for his son. But in all things it must exceed that had by the Dog of Israel. It must be more ornate, more beautiful—in design more superb, in aspect more breathtaking, in character more profound. Do you understand? No son of a captive king will surpass our own beloved prince Amêl-Marduk!"

Az bowed again. "I will apply my humble talents to this request as best I can. I will not rest until his majesty is pleased."

The agent produced another bag and poured it onto the scale where the amulet had rested. There was much more gold poured into the cup than usual. The agent placed the counter weights on the other side. Almost two minas worth of gold! Az's wife could not help but look at her husband with eyes wide open. It was nearly quadruple the amount of gold he was usually given for a task.

"As usual the king delights to honor his jeweler by paying in gold the same weight which he is asked to fashion." Az took the gold for the circlet and placed it in a leather bag. The agent then refilled the cup with gold coins until the weights balanced it yet again. Az emptied the cup into another bag, which he handed to his wife. She was smiling from ear to ear and had gone over to hug Az's mother.

"The king, our God, wishes his son to wear the gift for the celebration at the feast of Dumuzi. We will call again in two weeks' time." The king's agent spun quickly and marched dramatically from the premises, followed by his lavish entourage. He did not stay to hear Az mutter coldly, "You honor me."

His wife hugged him. "Do you know what this means? We have enough for the place on the street of merchants. We will live upstairs! And your shop will be below."

He smiled. "It is true. This, with our savings, will be enough to buy it without question."

His son-in-law, who had been outside listening, stepped into the small room and said, "This calls for a dance!" He produced a pipe. Az's wife took a tambourine and, by hitting her leg, began finding the rhythm of the pipe. His two daughters and his mother began to dance around the room. Az joined them with a silver flute he had made while he was in Egypt. It was a joyous occasion. At last—to live among the rich and prosperous of the city, to find the recognition as an artisan he deserved!

⇠ Chapter Three ⇢

Muruk looked at his friend and sighed. "You have a problem indeed." Muruk and Az had long been friends and seen more than their share of trouble together. They had grown up playing on the banks of the Euphrates; Az taking the part of Gilgamesh and Muruk, Enkidu. As children they had slain more monsters, tricked more gods, and defeated more warriors in battle than legions of heroes could have in a hundred years. Once they had floated down the Euphrates almost to Barsippa. It took almost two days to walk back, and when they returned their fathers had beaten them so severely—in gratitude to Ishtar for their return—that Az thought his father was determined to send him to Ereshkigal in the underworld. But this time the trouble was Az's alone.

"I warned you to stay away from metals, did I not?" Muruk shook his finger in mock severity. A slave came and refilled their glasses.

She was dressed in Egyptian linen and wore more gold than even Az had seen as the king's jeweler.

Az grimaced. "And I laughed when you said wool was the future after the fall of Nineveh. By the king's beard! Look at you! You live like the king himself . . ."

"Better!" Muruk laughed.

"Better indeed! You have slaves that own slaves, and they wear more gold and silver than my wife can even imagine wearing! It's fortunate the king's gaze is away from Uruk or I'm certain the tax collector would be here in a bull's breath," Az said shaking his head in disbelief.

"Bosh." Muruk laughed. "The king gets his share, I assure you. But there's still room if you'd just forget your 'art.' Wool is moving so fast I can't keep up. From Egypt to the Aegean Islands the demand is high. I could use a good man fluent in Egyptian."

Az laughed again. "You never quit! No, my hands are my gift from God, not my head. But I did not travel all the way to Uruk to hear more of your bragging. Come, you promised to hear the dream."

"So I did. Leave out nothing if I am to interpret it. Even the smallest detail can be important." Muruk stroked his beard purposely and looked at his friend with a deep, wise expression.

"The dream was even more clear last night. The thing is to be made of brass, the finest brass, like that produced in Athens. But though I can at least see the device dimly now, and its dimensions and aspect are becoming more clear to me each day, I cannot guess its purpose. And once made, what is to be done with it? One thing *is* clear. This dream comes from my God."

Muruk coughed and waved his hand impatiently. "My friend. I cannot interpret this dream unless I am told more about this new god of yours. I must admit you confuse me. You were Marduk's favorite. He has watched over and blessed you like few others. How do you turn your back on him in favor of this minor kingdom's deity?"

Az sat back and took a drink of the mead Muruk had set before him.

"You deserve the full tale. Sit back and listen—if you can manage not interrupting such a story."

Muruk waved him on and Az began. "I was returning from Egypt. Jehoiakim had just fallen and Jerusalem with him. The king of Egypt had just retreated past the great river and I was returning, along with several merchants, with some gold we had gotten at a great discount. War does strange things to a commodity's price. We were well defended and several groups had joined ours to bask in the safety of our large confederation of Babylonians, Israelites, and Arameans. I needed some contracts written and I hired a Hebrew scribe to do some work for me. He was a smart fellow, but with a rugged edge that I liked—very Babylonian, if you follow me."

"We had some long conversations late into the night. We talked of great mysteries, exploring questions about the stars and their course through the heavens. One of his ancient prophets had written great things about the stars and their purpose in the heavens. In our conversations he made known that he was a scribe to another great prophet to this God of Israel. The scribe's name was Baruch—an able and well-mannered man, but devoted to this prophet like no scribe I had seen in Babylon."

"He told of how their God had taken them, as slaves of Egypt, and turned them into a great and mighty people through unbelievable miracles such as dividing great seas, or fire from the heavens, or fighting battles for them when they were outnumbered and faced sure defeat. Of course, I've heard such stories all my life, of gods mighty and terrible that raised a hero or a people to great heights of glory according to their whim and will, but no story ever touched me like the stories that this man told. It seemed my heart had caught fire and my head was filled with the light of a sun that seemed to shine within.

"After three days of such conversation, I decided that I would make an offering to this God when we arrived in Jerusalem—to gain His favor. I told my plan to Baruch, thinking it would please him. Instead he just scoffed and said his God would not take such a sacrifice. This was not a God that one could satisfy with a sacrifice to appease or win His favor. This was not one of a pantheon of Gods, but this was the One God. The ruler of all heaven and earth.

"I asked what he demanded and Baruch leaned over, looked me in the eye, and said, 'Your life!' I was taken aback and replied incredulously, 'My life? He wants me to offer myself as a sacrifice?' Baruch had then laughed. He told me that no, not literally, but in a fashion, yes. This God demanded that I serve Him and Him alone, that my whole life and being be given for His purpose and for His glory. Then he told me something that struck my mind with such power that I wrote down the words. I still carry them with me, so let me quote them as I wrote them down fresh."

Az took out a small clay tablet that fit comfortably in his hand, then took a breath and continued. "He said, 'You asked if my God demands that you offer yourself as a sacrifice. No man can offer himself. You cannot offer your life, or another man's life, or even a thousand lives with any effect. But this God will do something which no god would dare do. This God—this God who created everything you see from the mountains that surround us to the stars you see in the sky—will offer Himself as a sacrifice for us. You see, this God is a Son. The Son of the Father of our spirits, and for us He will die. And He will do it for a reason which would be unheard of from the gods that you worship with their plans and schemes, with their petty jealousies and moods. The reason is love. This God will do it because He loves you. He loves all of us. Through His death we are redeemed We will live with Him forever!'

"I had never heard such words before—no I say that wrong. I have never *felt* such words before. They penetrated every corner of my soul. I felt their truth as much as I feel this cup in my hand, or feel the seat upon which I sit. They carried me away and I felt the love of this God. I feel it to this day. This God who will one day die for me, I've come to know is real, more real than anything I've ever known.

"Well, my friend, to make a long story short. Baruch immersed me in water in the name of this Son of God, His Father, and the Spirit which carries the love and truth of this God. He told me that he held the priesthood of one of their great prophets—one Aaron. At that time I gave my life to this God and His people. I promised that I would always remember the sacrifice that this Son would make and in so doing I would find mercy for my own transgressions and I would find forgiveness." Az stared into his cup as he said these last words.

"Your tale strangely attracts me," Muruk said after a moment. "I find a comfort in your words and seem to taste some of the light you describe in feeling these things."

Az looked up and smiled. "I find I cannot speak of these things without feeling again all that I felt. It is that Spirit of which I told you in whom I believe. Yet there is so much I do not understand."

"Have you not spoken again with this Baruch? Has he taught you no more?"

"Sadly no. When we arrived in Jerusalem, events transpired that forced Baruch from me. His prophet, Jeremiah—my prophet too—has been imprisoned by Zedekiah and Baruch had to go into hiding immediately. He was entrusted with sacred writings that had to be preserved. So there is much that I have not learned. Yet, still, I pray and think upon the things that I have learned. And now this dream comes again and again. I know that it is from this God—my God, but its meaning is unclear."

His friend refilled Az's cup. "Tell it to me. I have some skill in the interpretation of dreams. As you know, I was once consulted by one of the court astrologers on a dream of the king's." Muruk leaned back and was looking rather proud of himself, raising his cup for emphasis.

"Yes, yes . . ." Az laughed. "That is why I've come to visit you. I thought you might help clear these muddy waters."

His friend smiled and twirled his hand in the air, saying in a wise tone with a deep voice and an air of mystery, "Tell me the dream!"

"In the dream, I see a brass ball. Cut in half. It is covered with Market Egyptian—"

Muruk interrupted him. "Market Egyptian? Please, I must know everything. Explain."

"Yes—they use it for everyday writing. You've seen the glyphs of their walls."

"Of course."

"Such writing is too long and artful, so they have an abbreviated version to be used for everyday writing. Merchants use it quite a bit, hence, 'Market Egyptian.'"

"Yes, now I remember having seen it used. Can you read what it says on the ball?"

"No, but it is clearly Market Egyptian. The base of the ball, forming the bottom half, is perfectly round, and running along the inside edge of that bowl is a clear stone or glass that forms a rim around the inside. The center is dark, but rising from the ball are round, gilded bars shaped like the wings of birds. They rise and meet at a round hook like that on a lamp. The wings are narrow and you can see easily in between them into the darkness of the center of the bowl. The wings rise from the edges of the bowl, completing the sphere and giving the impression that the whole device is carved from a single ball of brass. It is beautiful beyond description. Attached to the crystal ring are windowlike frames that slide over the top of the rim. In these windows appear words of Market Egyptian that change and shift—the words seem to dance within the ball."

Muruk interrupted, "I don't understand this clear stone rim. Can you be more exact?"

Az picked up two bowls, one larger than the other, and set the smaller bowl into the larger. He then poured his drink into the larger bowl until the rim of the smaller floated slightly above that of the larger bowl. "See the space that forms between the two bowls?"

Muruk nodded.

"Imagine that rather than a space, there is a crystal or clear piece of glass filling that space. It is such in my dream. Attached to this crystal are the windows which hang over the moving rings, which rings run next to the rim of the bowl just as the space does. It is in the windows that the words appear."

"Are the wings that form the covering of the ball of any bird you know?"

"I cannot say. They look like any bird, but like the rest, fashioned from brass."

"Then what happens?" Muruk asked, stroking his beard meditatively—his eyes closed in thought.

"I seem to travel to a new place, or I'm brought to a new place. It is night in the early spring, deep in the desert, and I'm surrounded by court counselors, both rich and wise beyond reckoning . . ."

"How many?" Muruk asked.

"I'm not sure . . . several." Az continued, "There is a star shining in the eastern sky, so bright the landscape looks as if it's under a full moon. But there is no moon. We are all staring at the star. The counselors seem to be consulting maps and ancient texts. Then one of the men turns to me and asks, 'What gift will you bring?' And the dream ends."

Muruk leaned back with an air of mystery. "I am ready to interpret your dream."

Az looked at him, a little surprised with how quickly Muruk had come to his insight. "Go on."

"The dream is one that will make you rich beyond your wildest wishes, or even that of your wife," Muruk quipped with a wink. "This god of yours wants you to begin in the trading of brass. While not as valuable as gold or silver, I've been following some of the merchants coming through the kingdom and there is a very superior brass that is blended in Kosala, which lies east of here, as the bright star of your dream signifies by its lying in the east. This brass is as hard as steel and holds a polish almost like gold. If you were to travel there, as I see your god wants you to, and start trading, the world would be yours. You see the ball represents the world, a world made of brass. The Market Egyptian writing means that you should watch carefully our enemy's attempts to beat you to the market. Egypt will be your greatest competition. The wings of the bird of course mean that you should act swiftly, as in the flight of a bird. And the rich astrologers signify you will be as rich as a king!" Muruk settled back and folded his hands on his wide belly. "I have spoken."

Az shifted uncomfortably in his chair. "He wants me to become a brass trader? That's what all these dreams are about?"

Muruk did not answer right away. He was staring straight ahead and drumming thoughtfully on the table. He picked up his cup, but did not take a drink. He was looking at it closely, but did not seem to be focusing on the drink at all.

"Muruk?" Az finally interrupted the stare to bring his friend back to the business at hand.

"Brass! Of course! Why did I not see it before? With the war with Egypt in full swing and brass becoming more scarce than usual because of the disruption of Phoenician shipping lines . . . Of course! Brass could be the next wool!" Muruk had jumped up and was pacing the room. Several slaves had jumped up to attend him, but he waved them off impatiently.

"Muruk. I'm not sure that's *quite* what the dream means . . . I think that it has more to do with—" Az did not get to finish his sentence.

"Nonsense. Of course. It's so obvious it's a wonder I did not see it first. Brass! We'll make a fortune! Leave the details to me. You're not set up to launch a caravan to Kosala, but I am. You back me with whatever gold you've got and I'll throw in the rest. I can guarantee you'll quadruple whatever you put in." Muruk continued to ramble and would not cease arranging and planning for the remainder of the afternoon. By the time that sun had fallen behind the shimmering waters of the Euphrates, Az had agreed to turn over his gold savings to Muruk who would in its place bring back the finest brass manufactured on earth.

Chapter Four

The red rocks shimmered ahead as they walked solemnly back to Babylon in the dry heat of the spring sun. Az looked at his daughter walking easily beside him and at the six guards talking loudly with them. The king's guard! What a luxury. But then the king's jeweler must have his protection when he traveled, and even though the way between Uruk and Babylon was relatively safe, these warriors made the trip much more secure than it would have been. They were not happy of course and complained incessantly about not being at this battle or that battle, but most of these guards had passed their prime as warriors. Some had even served with the king in the battle against the Egyptians at Carchemish.

Az looked down at his daughter and she looked at him and smiled. He and Melon-Flower had a special relationship, and she was the only one in the family that had joined him in his belief in Israel's God. But they had always been close. Since she had been a little girl, she had been fascinated with all that her father did in his shop. She had helped for as long as she could remember, first just sweeping and cleaning, but lately, now that she was twelve, more important things like preparing the kiln or helping pour the hot molten metals into their molds. She longed to learn her father's arts, but knew it was not the custom. When she was old enough she would be made a bride and assist her husband in whatever work he did, whether it was tending goats or conquering kingdoms. She thought it odd that her father had not yet chosen for her a husband. Her mother was pestering him constantly about it, but he had put her off time and time again. She was not sure if she should broach the subject with him, but she too was growing more curious. Her mother had married her father when she was fifteen and in a few years she would be of that age herself. Some of her friends had already been betrothed to their future husbands. The walk was a long one and there was plenty of time to bring up a difficult subject.

"Papa?"

Az smiled at his daughter. "What is it my Melon-Flower? Tired already of walking?"

"No . . ." She hesitated as she strung out the no. "I was wondering . . ."

"What were you wondering?"

She could not do it.

"What is Mama going to say when she finds out you've pledged the gold for the house she wants just to buy brass from the kingdom of Kosala?"

Az laughed. "I will tell you what she will say. First she will call me a fool. Then she will curse her father for ever choosing me as a husband. Then she will start to cry, whereupon she will fall on the floor and cover her head with dust, declaring it the greatest misfortune she has ever endured. Then she will most likely throw something at me. Nothing of value, of course, but something she thinks needs replacing anyway. Then she will not speak to me for a week. Neither will my mother, and neither will your sister. I predict we will enjoy great peace for a week or more."

His daughter's eyes were wide. "Papa! Will they not believe Uncle Muruk's interpretation of your wonderful dream?"

Az chuckled and then looked as his daughter kindly. "I don't believe Muruk's interpretation of my dream."

"You don't?" his daughter asked. "But why did you agree to purchasing the brass?"

"That was a sly business move, little Melon-Flower. You watch, after the sale of the brass we will triple our gold." Then he grew more

solemn. "But more than that, I felt right about
it. It's not why the dream was sent, but . . . I'm
not sure. It just seemed the thing to do."

"Oh."

Ever since that trip to Egypt her father had
said things like this. He seemed to follow an
inner voice that guided him in ways no one
understood. At least her mother or grandmoth-
er didn't understand, but she did. She had
believed everything her father said. And she was
starting to understand what her father meant
when he talked about these feelings. She had
begun to feel things herself ever since she had
started to pray in the name of the Son, the
Creator.

Az looked down at Melon-Flower. "It's
hard to explain. But I feel guided by something
bigger than myself. I've never felt like this
before . . ."

"Not even when you chose my name?" his
daughter asked with just a hint of concern.

Az laughed. "Well maybe *never* is too
strong a word."

"Tell me again how you chose my name!
How you left the midwife and mother alone to
wait for my birth, and you walked along the
river and . . ."

Az smiled at his daughter and began
thoughtfully, almost to himself, "It was very

dry that year—the fourth year of a frightening drought. The Euphrates was just a trickle and all of Babylon was frightened. Even the great gardens were dry and withered. Everyone was afraid that we would not have enough food to last another winter. Many said that your mother having a baby at such a time was a bad omen. They said your mother was past her prime and that the baby would be cursed. They claimed that she should have eaten the mugwort root and rid herself of it. But she would not hear of it. She somehow knew it was a daughter, and despite the protests of our relations, she carried the child. It was a hard time. Food was scarce and expensive. What food there was, was sent to the army to supply the war. When I left your mother in her pains, the midwife said to me, 'Do not hope over much. This is the fourth birth I've attended this month and they have all been dead at birth. The gods have deserted us.'

"So it was with a sad heart that I walked along the banks of the Euphrates. As I walked along the dry sandy bed of the river, I spoke to the gods I worshiped before I discovered the One God. I asked the gods why life was filled with such sorrow. The once-lush reeds along the river were a barren, dry yellow, and the ribbon of water that ran small and lonely through the center of the once great bed was thick and brown. I could have jumped across the water's flow with ease, for a small streamlet was all that remained of the greatest river north of the Nile. I was about to turn back when something green among the yellow reeds caught my eye. I approached it with wonder for I had seen nothing green in ages. There, tangled among the dried rushes, was a melon vine, green and alive, unconcerned that around it lay nothing but dry devastation. On the vine I found a plump juicy melon as big as my head, and beside it was a beautiful, large, full, and delightsome yellow flower.

"I took both and returned to our home. The midwife was gone, but your mother was sitting up on the mat. Her long, tangled hair and pale face were streaked with moisture, but at her breast was a fat little girl sucking contentedly. A smile graced your mother's face. She glowed so brightly the room seemed as radiant as if it were lit with ten lamps. I looked at you, then at your mother, and handed her the flower. She held it to her nose and breathed deeply its cool, moist scent. I looked at the flower and at you, so beautiful and full of life, and an overwhelming sense of rightness, of blessing, flowed over me. I felt that all was right and all would be right. 'Our melon flower,' I whispered, and so your name was born."

Melon-Flower was beaming brightly. "And the rains came that very week."

Az smiled. "Yes. The rains came that very week. Those strong feelings of rightness had not returned from that time until I found the Hebrew God. I find such feelings often now."

They walked in silence for a few minutes. He looked at his daughter and smiled.

"It's these feelings that forbid me to rush off and find you a husband!" he suddenly declared, as if he had been reading her mind.

She frowned a little and he caught the disappointment in her eyes as she spoke. "But Father, I'll soon be old enough, and you and Mother have the most wonderful dowry set aside. I should not be surprised if you could capture me a prince!" She had blurted it all out before she realized what she was saying.

"A prince!" Her father laughed. Two of the guards joined in and one turned to her father.

"I would make a fine match for your little flower. And I could certainly use that dowry." The others joined in, laughing, but Az was not amused.

"Silence! You dogs are to serve me as you would your king. Would you treat a princess so?" The guard was silent. "I thought not," Az finished. "Do not speak of such things again."

Melon-Flower could tell he was very angry and an awkward silence fell on the company.

Az let the soldiers fall behind a little and in a quiet voice turned to his red-faced daughter.

"I'm sorry, Melon-Flower, the thought of one of those odious men . . . just . . . just . . . never mind. Don't worry. I have been thinking much harder about your marriage than your mother would ever guess. Daughter, it may be in a year or two I will want to leave Babylon and set up shop in Jerusalem."

She was surprised to hear her father say so, but said nothing.

"I long to go to the Temple regularly to offer up sacrifices to my God. That is the proper place of worship. I long to learn more about the God that I've embraced. And, well . . . I would like to find you a husband among the Israelites. You are a believer after all. What do you think?"

She put her hand over her mouth. "Papa! Really?"

"Yes, I think so," Az continued. "Just have faith, little Melon-Flower. I'm learning that this new God takes care of His own. I think He has something special in mind for your life too. Can you have faith, Melon-Flower?"

She nodded and reached over, putting her arm around her father, and the two marched

along the road toward home in warm silence,
each lost in their own thoughts.

⇌ Chapter Five ⇌

Az's prediction of his wife's response to his using the gold for her new home had been more than accurate. For two weeks she did not say a word. And now, after four months, his mother had finally started speaking to him, but her conversation was mostly about where she had gone wrong as a mother, and how she must have angered the gods to have a son that would treat her so. But after two weeks, life for his wife went on much as it always did. There was bread to make, clothes to mend, lamps to trim, gossip to be exchanged.

The king had been most pleased with the circlet made for his son and had commissioned Az to make a grander one for himself. Much to the jeweler's wife's satisfaction, their coffer of gold had begun to be refilled. And as it did, Az's favor in her eyes began to be restored; she was almost being civil to him.

The dream appeared almost nightly now. The center of the ball was finally clear to Az and he could see two, flat, spear-shaped spindles floating in the center. They floated almost on air, and although they floated freely, there was a firmness and steadiness in their movement that gave them a sense of purpose. He felt compelled to follow the direction in which they pointed—he deeply *desired* to follow them as if the realization of his greatest dreams lay in the direction the spindles indicated. But the star was unchanging; every night it glowed there in the night sky. And the question, "What gift will you bring?" haunted him continually.

The birds had just begun their morning chatter when someone yelling brought Az off his mat. As he tried to clear his head, he realized that the voice was calling his name. He stumbled from the room, throwing a robe around him as he moved to the front of the house.

"I'm coming!" Az yelled.

As he entered the center of his house, there stood Muruk. The king's guards had gathered at the front of the house and were crowded around the door, peering in to see what Muruk was singing about. For singing he was. As loud as a gong and twice as deep.

"Muruk! You're back!" Az was wide awake now and embraced his friend, giving him the traditional greeting kiss. "I was beginning to worry. You've been gone almost four months!"

"The best four months I've ever spent. And as for you, my friend, you are a rich man!"

By this time all the family had gathered into the room. Muruk reached into one of the bags and produced a large, round, yellow metal disk. It was as large as a plate, but was as thick as his thumb was long. It was obviously very heavy. He handed the disk to Az, who carefully turned it over and over.

"This is beautiful, Muruk. I've never seen such fine brass. It's wonderful."

"That it is, and I've sold most of it already. These are just a few samples I saved for you, the rest are being moved to a buyer in town."

Something about the metal seemed familiar to Az, but he could not put his finger on it. The metal captivated him though. He had seen brass many times, but nothing so fine. This seemed more like gold than brass.

Az looked up and laughed. "Then you've doubled my money?"

Muruk looked down at the ground. "Well, no. I did not quite double it."

A tension settled over the room that seemed to intensify around Az's wife and mother.

His mother spoke first. "Well, how much did you make? You've at least returned what he gave you, have you not?" His wife was trembling and his mother moved over to put her arm around her.

Muruk was staring at the floor and seemed a little ill at ease. "There are risks in any venture, and what with the cost of the caravan, moving the goods to and from here, unexpected losses along the way . . ." He paused as if afraid to go on. "So, considering all of that, I was only able to increase your money by . . ." Muruk seemed to let the sentence linger for much longer than anyone in the room could stand. " . . . by twenty-seven times!" he shouted at last.

No one said a word. Not even his wife hitting the floor with a thud seemed to move anyone from their statuelike trance. Finally, as his oldest daughter rushed to help her poor mother, Az found his tongue.

"Twenty-seven times? That's a king's treasure. Are you sure?"

Muruk laughed a deep, satisfying laugh. "I'm quite sure! That god of yours sent you a dream of dreams. Of course, my own portion was much more substantial, as I had more to invest, but indeed yours is twenty-seven times your investment and the brass you see before you. You are a rich man now!"

It wasn't the money Az was thinking of, however. It was not even of his wife who was just starting to wake. Staring at the exquisite yellow brass on his rough dirt floor, he recognized why it seemed so familiar—it was the brass of the dream. Then suddenly everything became clear to him. Like a flash flood, his mind was filled with the overwhelming task he was to accomplish. He was to make the device that had consumed his dreams for these countless months.

⇥ Chapter Six ⇤

Az's new shop on the street of merchants had attracted much attention, with its two guards posted outside the door and its central location in the heart of buzzing Babylon. And as the rumors of Az's wealth gained momentum, having one of Az's creations become a necessity for anyone of status in the kingdom. Az now had more orders then he could possibly fill, so he had hired two other jewelers, whose work he respected, to join him. They were Hebrew, some of the artisans brought up after the defeat of Jehoiakim, but he was disappointed if he thought they would be interested in discussions about their God. They were even worse idol worshipers than most Babylonians and had no interest in discussing things of a more spiritual nature. But they were good jewelers and they worked cheaply enough.

And, despite less-than-satisfying religious conversations, it still felt good to be among the city's elite. Az thought how much he hated living among the common laborers and artisans of the city. His neighbor next to the old shop had been a shabby leather worker—often drunk and often loud. Az realized that this was where he belonged, and he smiled with some satisfaction at the cleanliness and refinement of those about him.

Az's wife and mother had never been happier. They now spent their days shopping and buying bread rather than baking it themselves. They strolled the gardens of Babylon with the wives and daughters of others whose wealth allowed access to the parts of the city that were barred to the less worthy.

While they pranced through the city, however, Az was anxious about something that never seemed far from the surface of his thoughts. Under his shop was a small room he had named his treasury. And among the gold stored for his use, and the use of those he hired, sat an ingot of brass that haunted him like the demons of the underworld he remembered from childhood. Day after day it seemed to call to him as he fashioned the ornaments to adorn the elite of the city. It whispered to him at night, and haunted his thoughts as he visited friends and entertained customers during the day.

His dream had become even more vivid—the fiery brass burned into his consciousness. When he awoke, the memory of the dream seemed to sear its image into his soul. There was an urgency about it, and every day he swore that today he would begin work on the device. But every day it seemed that something would come up that demanded his attention, pulling him away from what he knew was of far more importance. Today was no different. Just as his shop opened, he'd intended to send a servant (of which they had acquired two since their move) to fetch the brass. But in strode none other then General Amasis, commander, second only to the king himself.

Az bowed low. "Your Greatness. I am honored that for you enter my humble shop."

Amasis waved off his kowtowing. "I've heard great things of you. I have a task, for which none but the king's own jeweler will do. My daughter is to wed and I would like you to make all of the ornaments she will wear." Amasis pulled from a satchel a clay tablet, upon which was written a list of bracelets, anklets, necklaces, circlets, and waist bands that would keep an army of jewelers busy for weeks. Az stared at the list and realized that it would be at least a month of hard work. Perhaps more. The thought of the block of brass in the treasury crossed his mind just for a moment before it was pushed out by the thought of providing a service to the great man that stood before him. Known as the king's right arm, this was a man of which legends were told. A warrior destined to become a godlike hero. A living Gilgamesh. Certainly it was an honor to work for the king, but here was a man after his own heart—a self-made man. This man had risen through the ranks and had distinguished himself in count-less battles: Nineveh, Carchemish, Jerusalem, and on and on.

Az bowed low again after looking at the tablet. "I can think of no greater honor, but, time . . . when is the wedding?"

General Amasis laughed. "Soon. On the day of the next moon. I will celebrate her wedding to my second in command, General Nabû, on the day of the festival honoring the god that has watched over me since my youth and given me victory after victory. You have slightly less than a month."

Az shook his head. "Your Grace, please understand . . . that is hardly enough time."

The general's face turned a bright red, his eyes began to blaze in a way that sent a shiver down Az's spine. "Then you refuse!"

"No, no . . . of course not," Az stammered. "Perhaps the king has an order before mine?

That I may excuse." Amasis's face was as hard as a desert stone and his aged eyes looked strangely fierce.

"No. The king's requests have been light. No doubt because of the excellence of the spoils you return from your campaigns." Az bowed again. "I will do it. If my forges must be lit day and night. Your request shall be honored."

The great commander relaxed. Amasis was a man accustomed to getting what he wanted. "I will pick up the order the day before the wedding." Then he leaned over and added mischievously, "And I pay better than the king!"

As the general left and passed the two guards (who were standing at attention so tall and straight that Az could not help but smile), Az stared at the tablet and began shouting orders. There was work to be done and not a second could be wasted.

At the end of the third day, Az was so tired he crawled into his bed exhausted. The wedding ornaments were moving forward, but it was going to be close. As he lay on the edge of sleep it occurred to him that he had not dreamed of the brass since he had taken the general's order. Perhaps his God understood the obligations he faced. That night he learned otherwise.

Az dreamed he was in his forge. He was working on an anklet and was carefully tapping away. A man stepped humbly into the forge. He was clothed poorly, like one of the shepherds hired to watch Muruk's flocks. He wore no shoes on his feet and his long hair seemed windblown and tangled. In his hands he held a small leather purse.

"We are closed until the festival of Adad," Az said, not looking up from his work.

The man did not move, however. He stood there waiting as if he did not hear, then replied softly. "I have work for the king's jeweler."

Az looked up. "Didn't you hear me? We are closed. I'm taking on no new orders."

"I have a work for the king's jeweler," the man said softly again. Az stopped what he was doing. Despite the man's appearance his voice pierced Az like an arrow. Az put down what he was doing and walked over to the man.

"I am sorry. Your work will have to wait until after the festival of Adad. I have an order from General Amasis." Az expected the name of the general to explain everything. But the humble man remained unimpressed.

"I have a work for the king's jeweler," he repeated firmly.

"Are you more important than the general of all the armies of Babylon?" Az asked sarcastically.

The man finally seemed to understand. He looked sadly at Az and asked meekly, "Then should I find another? It is a matter most compelling . . . and urgent."

"I'm afraid you will have to. I am far too busy. If you will excuse me, I must get back to my work." Az turned and walked back to the piece he was working on for the general. The man stared sadly at him for a moment and then turned to leave. As he reached the door, Az looked up. The aspect of the man seemed so sad and distressed that Az called out, "I am sorry. If you come back another time, I would be pleased to help you."

The man smiled kindly, and with a note of pity in his voice answered, "I am sorry too. By then it will be too late."

Az looked at the man as he retreated out the door, and as an afterthought called out, "Sir! What is your name?"

But the man was gone. Az looked out his door and there in the cold night blazed the star shining brilliantly in the dark sky. He heard a voice say softly, "What gift will you bring?" And then there was silence.

⇥ Chapter Seven ⇤

His wife, his mother, his daughter, his employees, even his servants all stared speechlessly at Az. No one knew what to say. It was clear he had lost his mind. Since no one had moved he repeated his words.

"Please prepare the forge to work with brass rather than gold. I am going to General Amasis to tell him I will not take his order. As a gift, I will give him those things which we have made already. But we will make no more."

His mother found her voice first. "Did you hit your head? Are you moonstruck? He will kill you. You'll be thrown into the king's dungeon! You can't tell a general like Amasis that you have just decided not to take his business. I don't even think the king would dare do that."

Iltani started weeping. "Doomed. We are doomed!" she repeated mournfully between her sobs. She stumbled over to the hearth and scooped up a handful of ashes and poured them on her head. Falling flat on her face, she continued to cry loudly. Az uttered not a word but quickly walked from his home.

As he walked, he reflected on the reply that Baruch had given when he had asked what kind of sacrifice the God of Israel required: "Your life." Today such a sacrifice might be required, but his decision was made. The disappointment of his God still rang in his ears from the dream. He would do nothing else until the object required of him was completed—if he still drew breath after talking to the general. He had not gone far when he heard a familiar voice calling from behind. He turned around on the dusty street and waited until his daughter caught up to him.

"Papa! Mother says you are going to die! Is it true, will the general kill you?" Tears were running down her cheeks, clearing a path through the dust that her hasty run through the street had covered her in.

Az gathered her up in his arms. His own eyes filled with tears at the thought of not being with his daughter as she grew to womanhood—to miss choosing a husband for her and the grandchildren that she would bear. He held her tight and she asked again. "Is the general really going to kill you, Father?"

He took a deep breath. "He may, but my God has given me a task. Perhaps He will protect me."

"It's about your dream, isn't it!" Her eyes lost their fearfulness, her look of terror replaced with one of hope.

"It is, Melon-Flower. I must get to work on making the device in my dream," he said softly.

"Then all will go well for you, Father. I believe in your God. He always watches over us. Father, the general can't kill you." She pulled away and began heading for home, but turned and, smiling broadly, added, "I'll go and say prayers for you."

If only he had the faith of that child!

His stomach felt twisted as he approached the general's palace, and his heart was beating so hard he could feel it throbbing in his throat. He gave the gatekeeper his name and waited while a messenger was dispatched to seek the general's will. Az was hoping the general would be too busy, or that he would be away on some errand of the king, or bathing perhaps. Anywhere, but at home and available. But he was to be disappointed; the messenger returned with instructions to take the jeweler to the general's table where he was dining with a few of his military advisors.

"Your Greatness," Az said simply, falling to his knees and prostrating himself as low to the ground has he could.

"Ah. Come in. Honored guests may I present the king's jeweler—the finest artisan in the world. He is making the trinkets for the wedding of your bride."

A large man dressed in the armor of a field officer stood and bowed back to Az. It was the general's son-in-law to be, Nebû.

"What brings you to my table, jeweler? Come have a bite of lamb. Have you finished your task already?" The general signaled for a servant to set a place at the low table. But Az raised his hands signaling that he did not have time.

"General . . ." Az took a deep breath. "I must decline the task you have given me. I have brought the names of several goldsmiths whose talents exceed my own. Please understand that it is a matter of utmost urgency or I would never dare beg to be released."

The general simply stared at him like a man trying to understand the babbling of someone whose tongue had been removed. Az had fallen to his knees again and had lowered his head, but he knew the submissive gesture would do no good. He could tell from the change in the rhythm of the great soldier's breathing that his anger had been kindled.

"You are refusing an order from General Amasis!? Are you mad? I have been treated with more respect by the pharaohs of Egypt!" Az cowered as he heard a sword drawn from one of the soldiers standing by the door. He stole a glance at the general and saw his face so red and twisted in hatred that he knew then that he would die. When the general finally found his voice, he spat, "Slay him." A guard moved swiftly to carry out the grizzly work.

Az looked to the sky and called out in a loud voice, "O God of Israel, if I am to be your servant, have mercy."

"Hold!" The general's voice boomed through the small room. The soldier stopped a few feet short of where Az was kneeling.

"Why did you call on the god of Israel? Speak swiftly." the general's eyes were still narrow but his voice had lost some of its edge.

"It is He that I serve. He has given me a task, that is why I cannot fill your order."

The general sat back down. "So, the god of Israel has called you into service. Tell me the whole tale. It may be that you will yet live. This god interests me. I have often thought of sacrificing a bull to him myself. Come sit. Have some wine, and if I believe what I hear, you will live. If not, you will die. "

Az came and reclined at the table with the other men. He was given a bowl brimming with the most delicious wine he had ever tasted. Once seated he held nothing back. He told the general of his dream. He described the ball in great detail, the star, the strange holy men following the glowing portent, and then he told of his dream the previous night, his required journey to Jerusalem, his daughter's faith, his family—everything he could think of to ease the mind of the general. When he was finished, the table was silent. Suddenly Nebû's voice sounded, cold and callous.

"I say kill him. Dreams?" He laughed harshly. "He must be made an example of. If our own people do not respect the might of the military, then how can we expect it from our enemies? Kill him."

The other guest had not been introduced to Az, but he was obviously a man of rank and position in the army. He looked coldly at Az and said derisively, "I agree. He was given a great honor and has spat it out like a dog. Slay him."

The general looked at his two advisors. He stroked his beard and said thoughtfully, "You are right, of course. He should die. But I will not go against his god. This god of our jeweler is more dangerous than we can ever guess.

Never have the Hebrews lost when they are in the favor of this god. He has done wonders that make our gods look like simpletons. Not long ago the Assyrian king, Sennacherib, attacked with an army that could have crushed a hundred nations. While camped outside Jerusalem, the army was destroyed in a single night. Not by an army of men, but an army so terrible that the survivors told tales that would freeze a man's blood. The stories abound. This god is dangerous. Look at this man. He knew he would die coming here! But better to face death than the wrath of his god. No, I will not touch a man who has been called to a work by this god. I know this god's reputation well; every general knows the power of this deity. If the Hebrew fools had not thrown the prophet of this god in prison, I have no doubt that our forces would have failed in taking the city." The general turned to Az. "So better to face your death than the wrath of this god, eh?"

Az looked up for the first time. He considered the men standing haughtily before him, their cups filled with rich red wine that stained their teeth; making them seem more like lowly animal scavengers then men. Suddenly the thought of the humble beggar of his dream seemed more majestic and noble than a thousand of these men who thought so much of their power and honors of the world. He rose to his feet and stated simply, "It was not fear that brought me here. It was love. I love this God more than I love my life."

The men stared in astonishment. Gods were to be feared, cajoled, tricked, honored, or venerated, but loved? The thought was so new they could not even comprehend it. The general was the first to find his voice. "Would that I had a hundred with such courage as you have shown. Babylon would stand for a thousand millenniums were it so. Your god must have some great task for you. There is some great purpose in this. I can feel it. Perhaps you are to make this thing to free the prophet that Zedekiah keeps locking up and releasing!"

"Perhaps, but whatever He asks, I must do." Az returned to his knees again remembering his place. The general paced for a few minutes and seemed lost in thought. The other two men in the room hovered menacingly over the jeweler who seemed to have caused such emotion in their leader. The general sat down and stared into his goblet for quite some time.

Then he arose and signaled Az to follow suit. "I release you. I will find another jeweler. I am leaving for Egypt in two months to collect the tribute from Necho in Egypt and Zedekiah in Jerusalem. If you would travel with me, I would be happy to escort you on your task." The general extended his hand and Az grabbed his upper arm as the general grabbed his.

All Az could mutter was, "Thank you. I would be honored to travel with your eminence and the army of the king of Babylon." And it was over. It seemed amazing, as he walked the crowded streets of Babylon, that not only was he still alive, but he had obtained the escort of the greatest army on earth to travel to Jerusalem. Truly this God he worshiped was a powerful ally.

⇥ Chapter Eight ⇤

When Az stepped lightly into his shop, his wife screamed in joy and flew over to him, throwing her arms around him and kissing his face, unashamed of the scene she was making. It seemed she was not yet a widow.

"Ha!" his mother exclaimed triumphantly, "I told you he would not go. My son may be a fool, but he is not that much of a fool."

Az roared with joyous laughter. "Mother! Would that every son had a mother that could make me laugh as you do. Of course I went!"

Everyone stopped talking and the place grew quiet. He went and was still alive? His daughter broke the silence. "I knew he would be fine. Our God was watching over him!"

"Yes, He was!" Az exclaimed. "And not only have I been released from the general's request, but he will escort me to Jerusalem when I am finished with my task."

His mother shook her head and began to chuckle. "You had me tricked. I thought you really had gone." She turned to the other members of the family and, shaking her head, said, "He did not go. He's having a little joke with us. And it would have worked too, if you had not added that part about the general escorting you to Jerusalem. Very amusing."

Az laughed again but did not try to argue with his mother. "Is the forge ready to handle brass?" No one said anything. One of the Hebrew jewelers he had hired looked at the ground and said, "We did not think you were coming back, and if you did, we thought it would be to complete the general's order."

Az was in too good a mood to be to unmerciful. The man's logic was impeccable; it was his faith that was lacking. "Then get to work, man, we'll be working only brass for the next month at least. We have a . . . a . . . something to make."

* * *

It was the best and worst month of his life. There were spiritual highs when he was sure the great God of Israel was guiding his hands and heart. There were days of such despair and despondency that Az was sure the task was beyond his skill. He allowed his employees a month of rest, with wages. He sent his wife, mother, and oldest daughter and her husband to visit with his uncle in Kish. Only his youngest daughter, who believed in his God, Melon-Flower, was allowed to stay and assist. Each day began with prayer. Az pled for guidance in making the device that would free His prophet, for surely that was what it was for. Ever since the general had suggested the idea that this strange ball could be used to free Jeremiah, the prophet of Israel, Az had decided that must indeed be its purpose. Somehow, Az marveled, he, an obscure jeweler, was being called upon to free the holiest man on earth. And he took his task very seriously.

Melon-Flower helped her father from morning till night. She worked the billows to keep the kiln blazing; she handed him tools; she cooked their meals and bought bread and supplies from the market. She did all this cheerfully with an air of fulfilling a mission and the sense that there was something very holy about the work in which they were engaged.

By the end of each day they were both exhausted, but slowly the object of Az's dreams began to take shape. Each night the Lord instructed Az through his nighttime visions, which had became very vivid and clear during this time, on each step of the process. It was like nothing that either father or daughter had ever seen; like nothing they had even imagined. Az watched excitedly each day as the object took shape. The basic design was a brass ball of perfect roundness. Around the equator of the ball ran a band of clear glass. Inside the lower hemisphere of the ball, within the ring of glass, were placed a series of nested rings made of thin brass placed one within another. Each ring slid within another smoothly and independently. In each individual ring were fashioned a set of windows of various lengths such that when the many rings were rotated, the windows would be arranged in a way to expose different parts of the innermost ring, which was without windows.

The nested rings were attached with rollers that allowed the entire ring to rotate smoothly and without a sound. Words in Market Egyptian were written upon the innermost ring. These Az placed in relief instead of carving them, which would have been infinitely easier. When different layers of the nested rings were turned, the windowlike frames could be moved in such a way that any combination of words could be exposed depending on which windows were open to the most inner ring, and which rings did not expose the inner ring. Through the glass, the exposed words written on the inner ring could be read through the windows. The words changed as the rings were turned, and as the window frames moved within the device, they framed new word combinations.

Every word he chose to place on the inner ring had been given to Az by the Lord through His Spirit. Az made each word of gold, then fused it to the brass inner ring. The rings had to be placed in tracks so they remained securely attached to the bowl frame. It was demanding, exacting work. When the complicated assemblage was ready, Az capped the lower hemisphere with a thin plate of brass so the rings were hidden.

Atop the plate which hid the concentric rings, Az placed two spindles. Of all the inglorious metals that could be chosen, the Lord had commanded one to be made of iron, but the other was of purest gold. The spindles sat upon a little post in the center of the device and were so perfectly balanced that they seemed to float in the air. He noticed that the spindle of iron seemed to favor a certain direction, but the one of gold turned freely—not so freely that it spun randomly, but firmly enough that with the most delicate touch it moved smoothly and easily, much like the inner rings that allowed words of Market Egyptian to be exposed on the side.

To top the lower portion, Az ornamented the ball with a tall lid of such enchantment that his daughter declared it the most beautiful thing he had ever made. He had to agree. For the top half he carved the twelve symbols of the tribes of Israel and the spreading wings of a seraphim. These he inlaid with gold. The lid rose to a peak and numerous thin lines were cut into it so the spindles were clearly visible. Then he sealed the rounded top onto the bottom half so that the spindles could not be touched. The effect was of a perfectly round ball with a band of fine, clear glass around the rim which exposed words in Market Egyptian, and a rounded lid ornamentally carved through which one could see the spindles.

It was late at night when father and daughter completed the device. It was strange that the Lord had provided no way to move the rings from outside of the ball to determine which words to expose. There also seemed no way to determine which way the spindles pointed. But despite these oddities it was a wonder to behold. For what purpose this was made he could not guess. It seemed such a beautiful and amazing work of art that he knew beyond doubt that he had not made it. It had been his hands, truly, his kiln, his Kosalaian brass, his Nimrudian glass, his tools, but the work was not his. His skill as an artisan was great, but it was not at this level—his mind could not have framed such a wonder. Other hands had used his hands. Another mind had enveloped his mind and created something far beyond his humble skill. He could only claim the same credit an anvil might receive for producing a king's crown. Truly this had been prepared by the Lord.

His daughter, in tune with his thoughts, fell on her knees and spontaneously began to thank the Lord for their blessings. Without a thought Az fell to his knees and joined her in pouring out his gratitude for letting them be a part of their God's grand designs.

Chapter Nine

The good-byes had been hard. Az's wife hung on to little Melon-Flower for as long as she could until Az pulled her away. He understood. No one traveled on a journey of this length without the risk of never returning. His wife had tried in every way to persuade him to change his mind and leave the little girl behind, but he fully believed that her prayers had saved his life, and it was her faith and help that had made it possible for him to make the device. She would not be left behind.

No one else understood this journey. Az's mother was convinced he had lost his mind. His wife just wanted things to return to the way they were before (but not before he had made his fortune with the Kosalaian brass). And it was hard to convince them of the import of the trip when all they could see was a small cedar box.

Both he and his daughter had wanted to show everyone the piece of work they had wrought together; they wanted to take it to the king and have it receive the praises of royalty. But something strange had happened the morning before his family returned. Father and daughter had left the device covered on a table in the foundry; when they returned in the morning it was just as they'd left it, except that inside the window the Egyptian message was clear: "Show no one."

Az immediately called his daughter to him with a trace of annoyance in his voice. But Melon-Flower held her hands out and said innocently, "I never touched it."

He turned back to the ball. "Then how . . ." He never finished the sentence and his daughter's wide eyes revealed that she was thinking the same thing. From that moment he had put it into a padded leather pouch, then placed the pouch in a cedar box filled with sawdust. He had allowed no one to see it. His mother and wife found this quite insulting, but he was firm. No one would look at it until it was shown to Zedekiah and he offered it in exchange for Jeremiah's freedom.

So now they were walking. The hot red sandstone lay as far as they could see. They walked in the rear of the army with several other merchants who had paid for the privilege and protection of traveling to Egypt with the

Babylonian army. The talk was of the asking price of barley and wool, the buying cost of wax, the continued rebellion of Egypt, and the quality of Athenian poetry and such things. Where Az would normally have joined them in their speculations and gossip, now he was full of anxiety and remained silent. He knew that he would eventually have to stand before Zedekiah, but how to approach this negotiation was going to be delicate. If he approached it badly, he could end up not only losing the brass ball, but his life and the freedom of the prophet as well. He would have to make Zedekiah think that he had some protection . . . Ah, that was it! He was the king's jeweler. He would say he wanted to show Zedekiah what he had made for the king, and that it was being protected by Nebuchadnezzar's army. Then, after the old puppet king had had a chance to lust after it, he would mention his conversion and his love of the prophet Jeremiah. Then he would offer Zedekiah the ball in exchange for the freedom of Jeremiah. That would be the approach to take. As long as Zedekiah thought Az was supported by the might of Babylon, he would not likely try to steal the ball.

But then, rumors out of the south seemed to suggest that Zedekiah was getting more rebellious, and though he had not turned his back on Babylon completely . . . the possibilities disturbed Az. Something was bothering him, though whether it was his plan or something else he could not tell.

Perhaps I could find Baruch and consult with him, Az thought. *That is what I will do.* So on he walked, envisioning meeting and freeing the prophet, meeting his old friend Baruch, and winning the praise of his God for the great work he had performed.

The journey took two weeks and was largely uneventful, but there was something magnificent about traveling with the greatest army in the world. Az stared at the soldiers marching around him, their bronze-plated armor scattering the sunlight. Except among the young recruits, few were without terrifying scars—their legs, arms, and faces marked with the savage wounds of previous battles—giving them each a fierce, defiant countenance. Their peaked, conical helmets rising to a point, their braided, squared beards, the metallic click of their swords, the soft thud of the butt of their spears striking the ground as they marched in laced sandals and linen kilts—all of this gave them an unconquerable demeanor that Az admired, and even envied. They carried provisions, as well as additional weapons like slings, bows, and arrows, with ease. Az was amazed that they could walk all day carrying the implements of war and apparently not tire (although he overheard not a few complaints from time to time). Ahead of the columns of foot soldiers rode the great cavalry, horsemen of rare skill and agility armed with bow and spear. These men were stern, proud, and daring. Az could not help but wonder what it would be like to face such men in battle. He suspected their visage alone was enough to put some enemy soldiers to flight. Az felt a strange longing to be a man of such caliber and strength.

Most glorious of all, he thought, were the drivers of the great war chariots. Leading the calvary, the chariots held the elite commanders, the lords, the princes, and the general's most trusted officers. The general himself rode in a chariot driven by four fiery horses, stallions strong and fearless. That well-crafted vehicle would allow him to drive from one part of the battle to another with great speed in directing the affairs of war. Surely there was nothing to compare with the army of Babylon!

Az walked in the rear with the merchants, the wives of the soldiers, and the logistical support of smiths, leather workers, carpenters, cooks, bakers, grooms—an army of people almost as large as the fighting force itself.

Among this group on the heels of the army appeared those Az considered the biggest danger on the journey. These were Aegean mercenaries—a rough lot lacking the discipline of the regular army. They spent much of the night drinking, fighting, and looking for trouble in the villages through which they passed. Az was especially worried about his daughter. She was now almost thirteen and nearly of marriageable age, and certainly old enough to attract the attention of men of the type who attached themselves to the army for pay. But since Az was a guest of the general, the men seemed to treat them with a modicum of respect. Nonetheless, Az kept an eye on his daughter, never letting her out of his sight.

However, he was grateful for the army's presence. It was strange to be traveling this far and not have the usual worries about bandits, zealots, and the ilk that preyed upon traveling companies. A small group was almost certainly going to be attacked. Even a large caravan would sometimes fall prey to a large organized band of thieves. But with the army of Babylon as their escort, there was not a force on earth that could challenge them. Not one.

Az spent almost every night in the massive and luxurious tent of the general playing games and talking about religion, the gods, and philosophy. But these talks always seemed to return to the God of Israel. Az described his conversion, and almost every night the general probed him for stories of this God and His works. They were nights never to be forgotten. A power attended their conversations that seemed to cause the lamps to shine all the brighter. Az discovered the general to be a very learned man; he asked difficult questions that exposed the heart of almost every topic he explored. The strange thing was, Az seemed to be able to answer these questions and even provide insights that were far beyond his ability to provide. In this he knew he was attended by a power beyond his own. The God of Israel was truly sending His Spirit to help him.

One night, as they neared Jerusalem, the general seemed in a particularly distracted mood. Az arrived as usual just after the evening meal, and the general ordered a slave to set up the game board. Az thought the general seemed more quiet than usual, but dismissed it as he watched the twenty-square game board being prepared. Amasis despised the simple dice games played so often by the soldiers under his command. He was, however, a master at many of the more challenging games. He was not bad at Hounds and Jackals either. He had a beautiful set carved from jet-black obsidian and elephant ivory, which, he assured Az, was once owned by the current pharaoh. He was also very good at Kalaha and Senet, both Egyptian games, but his passion was the ancient Royal Game of Ur. At this Amasis was unbeatable. That's why, as the evening progressed, Az thought it strange that he was so far ahead of the general in the game. Az already had all seven of his pawns on the board, and had removed three of the general's without causing the usual deep frown or furrowed brow that marred the general's face when it seemed he was falling behind. Az was excited. He had four of his pawns on refuges and was starting to hope he might actually win his first game since leaving Jerusalem. He was going to beat the general!

But Amasis was rolling the sheep- and ox-knuckle bones distractedly in his hands and staring blankly at the board. Or rather, he was staring through the board. Something was wrong.

Suddenly, he looked up at Az. "You say there is just one god. One god who created the world. One god who rules the heavens. One god that makes the sun rise. One god who watches over the fates of nations. One god who brings in the harvest. One god to do all things.

I find this impossible. Suppose you offend this god. To what other god do you turn? Suppose your sacrifices fail to please this one god? There are no options, nowhere else to turn."

The general paused for a moment and Az was about to say something, but Amasis continued.

"And not only that, suppose you are wrong? Eh? What then? If you sacrifice to several gods then at least there is a better chance that one will be able to help you. Before going into battle I always sacrifice to at least three or four gods, just to ensure I get the attention of at least one. Your faith is like a military commander that has put all his army in one place with a single plan of attack—with no chance to retreat, to call reinforcements, or to bring any flanking maneuvers into play. Placing all your trust in this single Hebrew god is not only foolish, but dangerous."

The general sat back and looked at Az expectantly. Az could tell it was his move and he chose his words carefully.

"You are right, if the choosing of gods is like a dice game. If it is just a matter of playing the odds, then your strategy is clearly the better. But suppose there is only one God. You have told me yourself of your impressions of the Hebrews' God. His prowess in battle. His destruction of Israel's enemies. He is a God of great miracles it is true, but He is more than that." Az paused to gather his thoughts. "I do not worship Him because of the miraculous events that I've seen—and I have seen many in my own life. No. I worship Him because He communicates with me directly. He guides my steps and opens the way for me. He is a God of not only large things like the courses of nations and the outcomes of battles, but He is a God of little things as well. A God who cares about my daughter's happiness as much as that of the kings and princes of Egypt . . ."

Amasis laughed out loud. "What kind of god do you worship? What? Does he care about the chamber pots and the contents of the cooking stove as well! Does he care about every straw in an old woman's broom? I have no use for a god of such minutia. Give me a god of strength. A god that embraces the virtues of courage in battle, of loyalty under command. Give me a god that Gilgamesh the hero of old could worship, not a god that fusses over the wishes and needs of a jeweler's daughter."

Amasis continued to shake his head and chuckle, but Az became earnest.

"You misunderstand. He cares about all of us not because He cares about the trivial . . . He cares because we are His children. His offspring. We are the sons and daughters of the Great Creator. We matter more to Him than the stars that spin above the earth, than the rivers, and the great oceans. We are His kindred. He cares about my daughter because she is His daughter as well. Do you see?"

Amasis had grown silent.

"That is why He cares about everyone. We are the children of this great God."

Amasis stroked his beard. "What a strange thought. You believe that everyone, even the most common beggar on the streets of Babylon, is in some way deity?"

Az waited while the general considered his words.

Finally the general smiled darkly. "I hope your religion never spreads far. That is a dangerous belief. What if everyone believed they were the offspring of a great god? Who could rule a people with such a belief? That would make a worthless beggar equal to a king. You keep this god. I will trust in a warrior's god who values a man by his strength, and who honors those who make themselves great."

With that, the general threw down the knuckle bones. Az lost two pawns and the game went downhill from there. Az lost again, but he left the tent humming to himself. Who would have thought that a simple jeweler would be playing games with the leader of the world's army, and on his way to visit a king no less; to visit a king in hopes to free a prophet. Az puffed out his chest and smiled as he returned to his own tent.

The days of debate and discussion passed all too quickly, and soon they reached Jerusalem. *At last!* Az thought, relieved. The city was much changed since he had visited before. Most of her artisans and princes had been taken north as captives in Babylon when she had been defeated by Nebuchadnezzar's army. The city seemed dirtier and less well-kept since the defeat of Jehoiakim and the departure of her elite. A few merchants remained, along with some government functionaries—or those that fancied themselves as such. But mostly the city was filled with the poor, those unfortunates that his king had not taken north.

As the army passed through the gates, he thought of the Jerusalem that he had visited with his father when he was a youth. The markets had been full. The city seemed alive with silver, gold, wool, and merchants. *What a change!* he mused. While Az looked about him, the general established his headquarters in Zedekiah's palace, and the army set up outside the walls, billeted in a tent city that arose within hours of their arrival.

Az entered the general's quarters to thank him. The general seemed preoccupied with his preparations to visit Zedekiah, but sent everyone away when Az entered the room.

"You have been a most intriguing traveling companion. I shall miss our conversations much!" The general was smiling and held out his arm for Az to grasp.

"I too will miss them. But, your grace, it has come to my mind that while you are here you should visit with some of the Elders of the Jews. They are much wiser than I, and I think would answer your questions more satisfactorily." Az reached out and took the general's arm.

"Perhaps. This god still intrigues me. One god. What a concept! It seems such an empty pantheon, but the idea is compelling—if it were true." The general sat down and motioned for Az to follow suit.

"I have a request to make of you, Az. Perhaps I have no right, but since I have protected it—and since you made it on my time as it were—I would like to see the device before we part. I'm most curious to see this thing your God has had you make to free your prophet."

Az hesitated. He knew what lusts could be engendered by beautiful things, and here was a man who could take it with ease. Az also remembered the warning written on the device to show it to no one. But that was back in Babylon, did the Lord mean now too? He also knew to resist would end fruitlessly, so hesitantly, and with a measure of doubt, he reached into the satchel that had not left his side and pulled out the bundle wrapped carefully in sheepskin. He handed it to the general.

The general gasped when he had exposed the mysterious object. "It is beautiful!" The general turned it over and over in his hands, examining the writing on the sides and blowing on the spindles to try to make them turn. "Magnificent. I've never seen its equal."

Suddenly a change came over the general. Az could not be sure what it was: a narrowing of the eyes, a stiffening of posture, a tightness in the mouth? But whatever it was, he knew the general was not going to give the object back. The general set it on a wooden table and turned to Az.

"Jeremiah will be freed. I will see to it. Zedekiah is the puppet of our king and I am the king's fist. I will retain this device. Your mission is successful. It is unfortunate that we did not see this obvious solution before you had taken such a long journey." Amasis turned back to the ball and waved a dismissive hand at Az. "You may go. Your mission for your god has been successful."

Az remained where he was. Could the general be right? Certainly that is what *he* had believed was the purpose for making the device, but something seemed wrong. This was not the way it was supposed to happen; he could feel it.

"Your eminence, please. I do not think this is the way events are to transpire." Az stepped forward to retrieve his treasure. "If I may just take it and . . ."

In a flash the general had drawn his sword and stepped between Az and the ball. "Back, Dog! The thing is mine. You have fulfilled the mission your god gave you. Now go!" The general's eyes were firm.

"But . . ."

"Go!"

Az did not budge, but he was shaking. "My God forbids me," he stammered.

The general glared at him, but did not move forward. He looked from the ball back to Az, then moved toward the object resting on the table. "And *my* gods bid me take it!" And with that he reached out to pick it up.

What happened then was inexplicable. There was a flash of light as the general touched the device, then he was thrown back violently as if he had been struck by the shield of a charging calvary soldier. The general stared in horror at the ball though it had not changed at all.

There was nothing in its aspect that would have hinted that it contained such power. A moment passed in silence.

"Take it away!" the general said hoarsely. He was shaking violently. "Take it away! Your god has triumphed. Go! Go quickly."

Az did not hesitate. He gathered the ball—somewhat afraid to touch it himself—and its leather wrappings in his arms and fled the building.

For two days Az and Melon-Flower stayed at an inn near the Temple. The tension from the presence of the Babylonian army was palpable among the inhabitants of the city. Az heard rumors fly up and down the streets, rumors of help coming from the Egyptians, or that the Babylonians would be pushed back and Israel would be freed. But Az's only concern was to find Baruch and ask for his wisdom and help in finding the purpose for his wondrous device. Would the general keep his promise after their less-than-friendly parting and free Jeremiah? Twice Az even tried to seek entrance to the palace to visit Zedekiah, and twice he was turned away. After two days the general and the army departed, but, to Az's delight and amazement, the general was true to his word—no doubt in fear of Az's God—and Jeremiah was freed from prison.

⇥ Chapter Ten ⇤

"Did you see the prophet, Father?" his little Melon-Flower greeted him at the lodgings they had taken in the great city. He gathered her up in his arms and swung her around and around until they were both dizzy and laughing.

"I saw him indeed!" Az exclaimed. "What a blessing. Daughter, it's true. He is a prophet. The Spirit taught me the moment I walked into the room. It was not a voice like with which we speak, but it was so clear a declaration that I could not deny its reality. It was like something broke through to my soul and said, 'This is the prophet of Israel. He who holds all the keys for this day!' I can't tell you exactly how it felt, but it was real and it was from God."

Az sat her down and walked over to a small wooden table set up on the floor of the one-room dwelling that they had rented near the Temple. Az had spent almost every day at the Temple, making sacrifices, fasting, and pondering over what to do with his glorious ball. On the table was a loaf of oat bread and some goat cheese. He sliced off a piece of both and walked back to his daughter.

"Will you thank our God for this food? I'm ready to end my fast." His daughter offered a humble prayer, then Az dug into his meal with gusto.

"Would you like some wine, Father?" she asked, already pouring it into a brass cup.

With a full mouth Az mumbled his assent and had the cup emptied in a single draft. She let him finish his meal before she began to pester him with questions about the prophet Jeremiah. She knew he had arranged to see him and was anxious to hear if he had found out the purpose for the ball.

"He told me that the Spirit whispered to him that it was made for a great purpose—that it would serve as a symbol even until the last days!" Az mumbled in an excited voice with his mouth still full of bread. But then he lowered his head and added, "But he had no revelation about what was to be done with it. Clearly, at least, it was not to help release him from prison, for that's been done. But he said the Spirit was silent on its purpose."

Az's daughter nodded. "What should we do? Have you received any answers to your prayers in the Temple?"

Az shook his head. "No, though I feel very close to the Lord. Receiving a copy of the writings of Moses and Isaiah from Baruch has been wonderfully enlightening. Jeremiah is working on combining all the writings of the prophets into a great work, or I should say he is redoing it. He'd taken all the writings from Adam to Moses and had combined them a few years ago, transcribing them onto plates of brass, but they disappeared shortly after Zedekiah was placed on the throne. They were put in the charge of a kinsman of the king's, but he was apparently murdered by a servant who stole the plates, and they have not resurfaced. The prophet is saddened, but believes that they are not really lost.

"But all this is beside the point. He has started the redaction again, and Baruch has given me a copy. It's wonderful! I must tell you the stories! There are stories about Adam, the first man, and his baptism; there is the rejoicing of Eve on our first parents' fall; there is the story of Moses seeing earths without number and of his terrifying battle with the evil one; and there is the story of the children of Israel being led from slavery in Egypt and of their coming to the promised land. It is fascinating, my child, just thrilling."

"Oh, that I could be taught to read." Melon-Flower sighed in frustration.

90   STEVEN L. PECK

"You could learn, I've no doubt, were you allowed. But I will tell you the stories. They are wonderful." Az cut another piece of bread and pointed it at his daughter.

"My favorites are the writings of the prophet Isaiah. They tell of things to come at the end of our world and of the coming of the Son of God in the flesh. Wonderful reading, my daughter—wonderful reading."

On and on Az talked, prodded on until late in the night by his daughter's questions. Together they read from the writings Baruch had given him until the lamp's oil was sputtering in the bottom of the bowl. Az smiled, noticing that Melon-Flower had reluctantly fallen asleep as he read out loud from the writings of Isaiah. Softly he picked her up and set her gently on her bed. He then put out the lamp and thoughtfully knelt upon the ground in the direction of the Temple. His heart was as full as it had ever been and he wept tears of gratitude for the things he was learning.

In the morning, Az had a sudden thought that he should take the device with him to the Temple. His daughter was still sleeping, so he left a little money on the table so she could purchase the night's meal, then he left quietly. The sun was not yet up, but there were people beginning their day; some making their way to the markets, some delivering goods to customers, a few making their way to the Temple, but few were going there to worship, he suspected. It seemed odd, but the people at the Temple did not seem to worship as he had learned from Baruch that they should. There were richly dressed priests who stood and declared the strength of Jerusalem and how it would never fall, and that their friends from Egypt would rescue them and that Babylon would be crushed very soon. The Temple was also filled with poor street vendors haggling for small household idols, some even for the worship of Baal, the old god Anu. This god seemed to captivate these people more than their own God, but was hardly worshiped at all in the rest of the world. True, the sons of Zadok were there sacrificing the doves and goats brought by the people, but the priests seemed rude and unkind, so unlike the God they were supposed to represent in the discharge of their duties. They seemed more anxious to receive their payment—something they'd recently begun exacting—than to help the people draw closer to their Creator.

Jeremiah came once a day and preached to the people of the upcoming destruction of Jerusalem and their folly in trusting in the arm of Egypt for protection, and Az was horrified as his prophet—these peoples' prophet—was jeered and shouted down by the local priests and citizens. Jeremiah had wept sadly and talked of the coming destruction, but the people refused to hear him. Az could almost feel the hand of God hovering above them, but their eyes were blind and their hearts seemed closed.

But regardless of all this, Az still came to the Temple. Despite the violation the great structure seemed to endure daily, there was a grandeur and magnificence that seemed to be calling the people to come back, back to the God that was once worshiped here in holiness and honor. It was here Az would find a quiet place in the outer court to pray and think. He was told in former years that he would have been closely questioned as to his worthiness, especially as a non-Hebrew and a Babylonian at that, but now he passed through courts without a single eyebrow raised in question. The Temple was indeed full of many foreigners, mostly sellers of worship objects, or herbs and other things to heal the body or to free one of evil spirits and demons. There were also magicians and soothsayers. It saddened Az to think that this once great people, the very chosen of God, had stooped to this level of debasement. He shook his head and walked in sorrow. The voices of hypocrites surrounded him, and he realized this was not the people he expected to encounter in his newfound worship.

Az found a quiet place to pray and reflect on the far side of the outer court. There were a few humble beggars camped there, but it was not hard to find a place where he was largely undisturbed. He knelt and laid his burden on the ground.

"Show me the way, Lord," he pled. "Help me find some direction for your quest, some hint as to what should be done with this object."

As he prayed, Az suddenly felt very depressed. More so than he could ever remember feeling before. This quest suddenly seemed a hollow, worthless venture. His time and money had been wasted. There was no purpose to this thing, clever as it looked, as beautiful and wondrous as it was. It was a shallow, worthless thing—of no use to anyone. How could it be? Two pointers spinning uselessly in a gold-trimmed ball with Market Egyptian scribbled all over the side in moveable bands—it was a silly waste of time. He tried to pray harder, to make the feelings depart, but the heaviness continued and pressed upon his mind like a palpable weight. He had wasted his time. He had been tricked by feelings and dreams that were worthless and of no account. He had dragged his daughter through hundreds of miles of desert only to realize what a fool he had been! Dreams? Feelings? What were these to base such actions on?

Az started to cry and got off his knees. Sitting upon the ground, he stared at his hands. What was he doing in the fallen Temple of a poor and scattered people? Look how their God had left them—with a puppet king and most of the artisans and noble youth taken captive to Babylon. He looked at the bag of leather beside him. *I should just toss it over the wall and let it fall into the brook . . . No, I'll sell it!* Did not the general of Babylon lust after it enough that he was almost willing to slay Az? Perhaps he could offer it to the king. Zedekiah was known to have a taste for fine things. Perhaps he could get enough to trade for some things in Egypt.

But then he thought of the things he had read in the writings of the prophet Isaiah. Was not the condition of the Lord's people predicted there? He thought of his own feelings of hope as he sat day after day and read the sacred writings. He returned to his knees and said aloud, though in a meek voice, "My great God, in the name of thy Son who will come, even the God of Israel, please help me see clearly your plan for me. What is this thing I've made? Where should I go? Who should receive this humble gift that I've made?"

As he spoke a great calm filled his heart. The depression vanished as he mentioned the Son. Az opened his eyes and looked at the bag beside him. Instead of seeing a foolish, empty work, he saw a work of substance and purpose. He opened the bag and pulled out the ball. Written on the side were the symbols in Market Egyptian: "Well done, servant. Go." And one of the spindles was pointing south. He knew at last what he must do.

Chapter Eleven

The wind tossed the desert sands, stinging their faces. It was the second such storm in two days, but Az counted it a sign he was going the right way. *If the forces of nature are combining to keep me from going this direction, it must be right,* he mused. But even more important, the spindle had not failed him since leaving Jerusalem. It had pointed unfailingly the direction he was to take, and the direction was often surprising.

On the morning he was readying the camels he had purchased for their departure, Jeremiah and Baruch had stopped by, saying they had felt impressed that he would be leaving that day. The visit was short as Jeremiah was leaving for Egypt in a few days and there was much work to complete on his sacred history of Israel. The prophet was still working on abridging and organizing the writings of Moses and had found a beautiful account of the creation he wanted to integrate into the text before he left. After saying good-bye, just as he was about to depart, the prophet turned thoughtfully back to Az.

"Would you like a blessing?"

Az was astonished. This was the prophet. "I would be more honored than I can express. Thank you."

Jeremiah placed his hands upon Az's head and, after invoking the great priesthood, spoke words of great comfort and satisfaction to the trembling Babylonian. Az was told that he was on God's errand and that as long as he remained true to the directions given him by the ball, he and his daughter would return safely to their home, no thieves or robbers would notice their passing, and the elements would assist them in unexpected ways.

At the end of the blessing was a strange warning, so strongly communicated to his heart that he remembered every word: "My son, you must have faith that the things you feel impressed to do are the things the Lord would have you do. Should you fail in this task or choose roads other than those you are directed to take, the promises given are revoked and you will be on your own, like a bird blown into the desert. Be true."

Indeed the blessing had been fulfilled in marvelous ways. On the third day out of Jerusalem they approached a place where the road had passed through a narrow canyon. Az had been warned by several of the caravans he met that he would be a fool to pass there unprotected, but there was a sense of urgency in this quest, a feeling that he must press on and not wait for a larger party to join. As he entered the canyon, he saw a man standing like a sentinel near the entrance. He was dressed poorly and wore a large Egyptian-style sword. On his arms gleamed gold, and everything about the man spoke of danger. But as they passed, the man did not look at them once. The thief just stood staring off into the distance as if he had seen nothing. A few hundred leagues down the road a band of men of similar ilk were camped. They were playing games, practicing sword play, and drinking. They looked savage and cruel. Az could hardly breathe as the camel upon which they sat plodded past this gang of thieves. Melon-Flower hid her face in the folds of her father's robes and hugged him tightly; he did not dare to take his eyes off the two camels they led behind them, which carried their supplies. They seemed to be making enough noise for a herd of camels. Suddenly two of the men playing a game looked up and stared at them. Az met their stares, knowing the fear he felt could not be hidden. He almost spoke, but the men turned away and went back to their game. When they had passed, Melon-Flower looked at her father. "I thought they would kill us, Father. I've never seen such horrible men."

Az looked down at his daughter. "Truly we are on God's errand. I thought they would kill us too. They would have—without a thought. But I think they did not even see us. Like the wind through a palm they may have felt the whisper of our passing, but they could not grasp it." He laughed out loud. "And what a treasure they missed!"

Az had just convinced himself that they were on the way to Egypt when the spindle pointed more southerly. There was no road going that way, and, according to his knowledge of this part of the world, there was absolutely nothing in that direction. It was wilderness, largely unexplored, uninhabited, and untraveled, and yet the spindle clearly indicated that it was the way to go.

"Well, daughter," he sighed, "here is another test of faith. Do we go on and hope for a road heading that way, or do we just plunge into the wilderness? Our supplies are fresh from that last village. We have water for a week, but no more. What do you think?"

Melon-Flower looked scared. The wilderness was the place every city dweller feared. It was a place of lions, ostriches, and other beasts conjured up in stories told late at night—in particular, for misbehaving children.

"I don't know, Father. Who could be down there? Why would the Lord lead us to a place where there are no people?"

Az thought for a while, then stood, dusting himself off. "I cannot even guess. Perhaps we will travel to the sea and meet a great king sailing the world. Perhaps we will find some nobleman from Enoch's departed city. I cannot guess. But the spindle says go, so we must go."

The journey now turned from the terror of dangerous men, to the fear of wild beast; from the risk of robbery, to a danger of hunger and of being lost, but the spindle led them on. It did not waver. For two weeks they traveled southward. The spindle seemed to lead them to every spring in the desert. They found plants to eat, and even a honeybee hive in the cavity of a lonely acacia tree. But even given these blessings their food supply was running thin and Az became worried. He reflected again and again on the words Baruch had first said to him about what his God expected: *Your life!* He was ready to give his life, but he regretted bringing Melon-Flower along. She was so young. Surely his God would not require her life. He should have left her in Babylon, or at least in Jerusalem. But it was too late, and on they wearily traveled.

The device pointed steadily ahead, never
veering from the straight course it had set for
them. The desert seemed endless. The sand,
interrupted only occasionally by bare and wiz-
ened shrubs, seemed like an ocean of desola-
tion. Even the camels seemed weary and plodded forward sluggishly. The animal skins holding their water had been squeezed dry that
morning, the last few drops of their precious
water failing to alleviate their parched throats.

"I'm thirsty," Melon-Flower complained
quietly.

Az did not answer. He looked at her sor-
rowfully. Why had God taken them into this
trackless waste? He felt a hollow depression set-
tling over him. The sun was lowering and the
desert stretched forward unending until it met
distant hills in the horizon. His thirst was great
and he felt hot, fatigued, and frustrated. He
stopped his camel.

"What's wrong?" Melon-Flower asked. "We
can't stop here. We've got to find some water."

"I don't think we can make it to those
hills," Az said simply.

"Father, we have to. It's the most likely spot
for a spring."

"I don't think this is the way it's supposed
to be. We are following the Lord in everything.
Everything! Didn't the prophet say the Lord

would open the way? Remember the song that King David wrote? 'I shall not want,' it said. But this is too hard. I *do* want. I want water. We *need* water." Az seemed to be muttering to himself. "Everything about this is too hard. It seems to me that if we were really on God's errand, things would go more smoothly."

Melon-Flower climbed down and sat by her father. He could tell she was struggling too.

"Maybe we need more faith," she said guilelessly.

"Let's pray," Az said wearily. He lowered his head and asked simply that God bless them with water.

Both travelers opened their eyes and looked to the sky, fully expecting a dark cloud bursting with water to pour over them. The deep blue was unmarred by even a wisp of white. Az got up and explored the area, thinking that perhaps he should see if there was water nearby that they had missed. There was none.

Az sat down next to Melon-Flower. "We must be patient. We will wait here until we see the blessing and miracle of the Lord bringing us water."

They sat in silence for what remained of the day. When night fell they did not unpack the camels but sat in the shade of a rock, back to back, waiting. By midnight their mouths were so dry that they could not speak, and Az's tongue felt swollen.

Near dawn he looked at his sweet Melon-Flower, picked her up, and sat her on the camel's wooden saddle. He climbed aboard his own. His mouth was too dry to make the clicking sound that would move the camel forward, so he resorted to clapping his hands. The camels moved forward reluctantly.

Wordlessly they sat on the camels, rocking gently to the beasts' rhythmic gait. The day passed in a fog of semi-consciousness. Az had strange dreams. In every one of them, he was drinking, and splashing and playing in clear, cool water. But when he woke up he was still suffering greatly from thirst. He looked over at Melon-Flower and it occurred to him that he should check on her, but the energy would not come, and he slipped time and time again into dreams of rich springs of cold water before he could finally bring himself to move.

Night had come. Through his mental fog Az thought it odd that they did not stop to make camp for the night, and vaguely wondered why they were still journeying so late, but the camels were plodding forward despite the darkness. Were they picking up speed? Strange. He slipped into another dream. In this one he was hanging over a cliff on a steep slope. Below him he could hear water splashing and strange slurping noises, but he could not see where the noises were coming from. In the dream Melon-Flower was calling to him. "Father, water. Water, Father." Suddenly something wet his lips. He sputtered in confusion, then drank deeply. Melon-Flower was holding a gourd to his lips. It was no dream. He had slipped off the camel and Melon-Flower was pouring a cup of muddy water into his mouth. Nothing had ever tasted better.

The camels were still drinking as he got his bearings. They were at a tiny spring where rich rushes grew around a pool of water no wider than the span of his arms. The camels must have found it on their own. Melon-Flower looked at her father and smiled. "God answers prayers." Az nodded, but he felt a little frustrated and he couldn't tell if it was because he had doubted or because the Lord had taken so long to answer their need. They had almost died. Wasn't there a better way to answer prayers? It seemed strange that the Lord would treat someone who had walked with generals and prophets so harshly.

They stayed two days at the spring and then continued their journey. After five monotonous days, tired and weary, they came to a valley which contained a small rivulet. As they looked down, they saw below them a nomad's camp.

⊰ Chapter Twelve ⊱

"Father should we talk to them?"

Az looked at his daughter and smiled. "I think we should. But let me check our marvelous ball to be sure. It would be nice to stop, rest, and talk and trade with them, but they may be dangerous. Remember, Melon-Flower, these are not the kind of people we want to stay long with. These wanderers are usually a dirty and unsavory lot, not at all the kind we want to associate with. And at all costs say nothing about our errand."

Az removed the ball from its leather covering. Strangely the spindle was spinning as if the camel ride had loosened it. It spun slowly and then stopped, but Az had ceased looking at the spindle. The writing had changed! For the first time since leaving the Temple, the writing conveyed a different message. The words sent a shudder of disbelief down Az's back: "What gift will you bring?"

He stared in horror at the writing. What did it mean? Leave it *here* as a gift? Could the glorious star have portended this? Leave an object of such wonder and beauty with desert dogs? These people probably spent their lives wandering—poor and superstitious. These were nomads, beggars of the desert. What would they do with such a device as this?

He suddenly turned to his daughter and snapped, "Have you been playing with this? Was it dropped? I think you've broken it."

His daughter stared at him in surprise. "I've never touched it. It hasn't left the saddle bag since you took it out this morning to check the direction."

"Well, something is wrong with it!"

"Why?"

"Never mind. I'm going to get a closer look at these people. Stay here."

Az stomped off along the rim of the valley to get a better look. He backed the camels up so that they would not be seen and snuck as quietly as he could to a large rock near the camp.

The tents looked like they might have once belonged to a wealthy merchant, but they now looked weathered and worn. The people looked no better. It appeared to be only a small kin group consisting of three generations. An older couple sat by the tent door. The man Az assumed to be the patriarch appeared to be reading costly looking metal plates. His wife was mending. A younger mother was holding a baby and some young men were skinning a wild goat. *What a strange group,* Az thought as he looked down. Here was the patriarch reading a brass codex that looked like it was worth a king's fortune. One of the young men standing nearby, a large strong-looking lad, was wearing a sword that was of such beauty and worth that it even dazzled the jeweler's eyes. The hilt was of gold wondrously carved and ornamented; it was also richly inlayed with gems. Next to him was a bow of . . . *It could not be!* Az thought. *Steel.* Such metal was highly prized and the makers of such were a small and secretive group. How could such a band of wanderers obtain such treasures? Yet, other than these shows of ostentation, the group looked worn. Their clothes looked shabby from weeks of use and hung limply from their shoulders. Their animals looked thin and well-traveled and everything about the group cried out poverty of both mind and body.

Suddenly his suspicions of their lowness were confirmed. Several women gathered some of the meat from the butchered animal and began pounding it. After some time of watching this the patriarch called the group together and offered a blessing over the food—to what unknown god Az could only guess. After the prayer the members of this party began to eat the meat, raw. *Raw!* Az was horrified. His stomach churned within him and he fled back to his daughter.

"Get ready. We must go. We will not stop to share a meal with these swine. They are thieves. They have taken riches such has I have scarcely seen, and I'm sure they will do it again. Desert dogs like I've heard of all my life, and they are eating their meat raw. Come, let's go."

"Raw?" Melon-Flower made a face.

"Raw," Az repeated. "They look dangerous and well-armed. Let's go quickly."

"Where father? What does the ball say?"

Az picked it up, and to his horror, the writing had not changed and the spindle was firmly pointing at the family.

"It's broken. Something is wrong. Let's go back the way we came and camp again where we did before. We need to think."

Az was heavy-hearted as they walked back through the desert. It seemed impossible to move his feet forward. The Spirit that had so long accompanied him since the journey began was gone, and the heavy blackness he had felt at the Temple in Jerusalem returned. Every step forward seemed a burden. Even Melon-Flower felt it as she sat in the saddle, silently staring ahead.

What gift will you bring? The thought echoed through his mind

That night they made a cheerless camp. Melon-Flower started a fire and they roasted some ostrich eggs they had found a few days before in the desert. Az thought about their trip; all the miracles, safety from thieves, fresh water, food as they needed it . . . all for what? Had it been a dream? Was his wife correct, had he been touched by madness?

Nomads! Why did the device quit working just then? Why not yesterday so he wouldn't be mislead into thinking that the Lord really wanted him to leave it there? Why did the words have to be something that made so much sense at that moment, but were clearly impossible?

Melon-Flower handed him his egg, but he could not eat it. His stomach was twisted in knots. He pulled out the ball and looked at the writing. It had changed, but the words were random and made no sense. The pointers seemed to meander loosely as if the ball really had been dropped. Az put it back in its bag and walked over to the fire.

"Father? What happened? I feel like crying and I don't know why. Those wanderers must have been wicked thieves. I have felt heavy and sad since we saw them."

What gift will you bring?

Az just nodded and returned to his own dark thoughts. *Should you fail in this task or choose roads other than those you are directed to take, the promises given are revoked and you will be on your own.* The words of the blessing echoed in his head. But he fought them.

What gift will you bring?

"They are vagabonds!" he said out loud. "They are nothing! This thing was made for a great purpose. It was made for kings, not beggars and thieves. I must have taken a wrong turn. I wasn't listening closely enough yesterday. That's the problem; we have to go back until the thing is working again. We have got to . . ."

What gift will you bring?

Az sighed. He knew what he was supposed to do. But it was too hard. Could everything he had dreamed about the device be wrong? Was it not made for a great purpose? This was not how the task was supposed to end—leaving the ball with strange and wild people. It was supposed to be given to a king, a prophet, or even an angel. Anyone but these nomadic wanderers.

What gift will you bring?

"Father," Melon-Flower spoke softly. "You were supposed to leave it there weren't you?"

Az could not deny it.

"Yes. I think it must be so. But I cannot. I've been through too much. How can I leave it with . . . with them?" He waved a hand in the direction they had come. "It is too important to be tossed away like that."

What gift will you bring?

Melon-Flower looked at her father as his eyes filled with tears. She walked across the soft sand and picked up the bag and gave it to him. Az looked deeply into his daughter's eyes and nodded. He understood. This was not his mission. He was only the servant. He got up and dusted himself off. He stared at the stars shining above him and thought of the one shining in his dream. This would be his gift.

The round, full moon was just starting to rise above the horizon of the desert, casting long shadows over the rough terrain. Az patted his daughter's head with a sigh and started walking toward the nomad's camp.

"I'll be back by morning," he called over his shoulder and for the first time that day he smiled.

* * *

And it came to pass that as my father arose in the morning, and went forth to the tent door, to his great astonishment he beheld upon the ground a round ball of curious workmanship; and it was of fine brass, And with the ball were two spindles;

and the one pointed the way whither we should go in the wilderness.

(1 Nephi 16:10)

❧ Bibliography ❧

Arnold, B. T. "What Has Nebuchadnezzar to Do with David? On the Neo-Babylonian Period and Early Israel." *Mesopotamia and the Bible: Comparative Explorations.* Eds. M.W. Chavalas and K. L. Younger, Jr., 330–335. Grand Rapids, Michigan: Baker Academic, 2002.

Keller, W. *The Bible as History,* 2d ed. New York: William and Morrow and Company, Inc., 1981.

Landau, E. *The Babylonians.* Connecticut: Millbrook Press, 1997.

LDS Standard Works and contained reference material. Salt Lake City: The Church of Jesus Christ of Latter-day Saints, 1981.

Morrey, P. R. S. *Materials and Manufacture in Ancient Mesopotamia: The Evidence of Archaeology and Art.* BAR International Series 237. Oxford, England: British Archaeological Reports, 1985.

Neusner, J. *A History of the Jews in Babylonia, vol. 1: The Parthian Period.* Atlanta: Scholars Press, 1999.

Perdue, L. G. "Jeremiah." *The HarperCollins Study Bible: New Revised Standard Version.* Ed. W. A. Meeks, 1110–1207. New York: HarperCollins Publishers, 1989.

Pollock, S. *Ancient Mesopotamia.* Cambridge: Cambridge University Press, 1999.

Roth, M. T. "Law Collections from Mesopotamia and Asia Minor." *Society of Biblical Literature.* Atlanta: Scholars Press, 1995.

Saggs, H. W. F. *The Babylonians: A Survey of the Ancient Civilization of the Tigris-Euphrates Valley.* London: The Folio Society, 1988.

Swisher, C. *The Ancient Near East.* San Diego: Lucent Books Inc., 1995.

Vargyas, P. *A History of Babylonian Prices in the First Millennium BC: 1. Prices of the Basic Commodities.* Heidelberg: Heidelberger Orientverlag, 2001.

Von Saldern, A. *Ancient Glass in the Museum of Fine Arts Boston*. Connecticut: Meriden Gravure Co., 1968.

⇒ About the Author ⇒

Steve Peck is Assistant Professor of Integrative Biology at Brigham Young University.

He is a graduate of Brigham Young University (BS), University of North Carolina at Chapel Hill (MS), and North Carolina State University (Ph.D). He has published more than thirty scientific papers. His work has also appeared in *Newsweek,* the *Ensign* and the *Friend.* His poetry has appeared in *BYU Studies, Dialogue,* and *Billowing Ark.* A chapbook of his poetry, called *Fly Fishing in Middle Earth,* was published by the American Tolkien Society.

With his wife Lori he has five children who keep him busy and excited about life.